Adapted by S. E. Heller

SCHOLASTIC INC.
New York Toronto London Auckland Sydney
Mexico City New Delhi Hong Kong Buenos Aires

ISBN 0-439-37212-7

Designed by Carisa Swenson

12 11 10 9 8 7 6 5 4 3 2 1 2 3 4 5 6 7/0

Printed in the U.S.A.

First Scholastic printing, April 2002

CHAPTER ONE

Forbidden Fruit

Pikachu sniffed the air. The little yellow Pokémon smelled apples.

Ash Ketchum smelled the fruit, too. He was Pikachu's trainer. Ash was on a mission to become the world's greatest Pokémon trainer. Pikachu was helping him. They traveled with

Ash's friends Misty and Brock. Misty held her baby Pokémon, Togepi.

"These apples sure look good!" said Ash. "Let's go, Pikachu!"

Pikachu and Ash ran into the orchard to get some of the fruit.

"Ash!" yelled Misty. "You cannot eat that fruit. It is not yours."

Ash knew that Misty was right. Someone must have worked hard to grow these apples. It would be wrong to take them without asking.

But Pikachu had run into the orchard. It was too far away to hear Misty. But it did hear a strange noise in the leaves. Apples were disappearing!

"*Pika?*" Pikachu wondered what was happening.

Ash, Misty, and Brock heard the strange sound, too. They ran

toward it. There was Pikachu. Apple cores had fallen all around it.

"Pikachu!" cried Ash.

"*Pika,*" Pikachu shook its head. *I did not eat these apples!* The little yellow Pokémon pointed to

the trees. Another apple fell. It dropped into Pikachu's hands.

Suddenly, a net flew through the air. A girl came running. She had caught Pikachu in the net!

"So you are the thief!" yelled the girl.

"*Pika pika!*" cried Pikachu. *It was not me!*

Ash knew that Pikachu was not to blame.

"Pikachu did not steal these apples," Ash told the girl. "Look at the bite marks. They are small.

Pikachu's teeth are too big to make these marks."

The girl looked at the teeth marks. It was true. "You are right. I am sorry I yelled at you."

"*Pika,*" nodded Pikachu. *That is okay.* Still, Pikachu wondered who had eaten the apples.

CHAPTER TWO

Apple Thieves

The girl invited the friends for a snack. Her name was Ange. She was in charge of the apple orchard.

"It is hard work," Ange told the friends. Now that the fruit was ripe, she had to keep watch all the time. That is why there were

noisemakers in the trees. The sounds warned Ange when someone was stealing her apples.

"Do you run this orchard all by yourself?" Ash asked.

"Yes," Ange replied. "It is hard during harvest time."

"I have an idea. Since you gave us some apples, let us help you out in the orchard," Ash said.

"Oh, thank you!" exclaimed Ange.

Ash, Misty, Brock, and Pikachu followed Ange on a tour of the orchard.

At the same time, Pikachu's enemy, Meowth, was taking its own tour. The talking Pokémon belonged to two teenagers, Jessie and James. The group was called Team Rocket. They were always trying to steal Pokémon for their boss . . . especially rare Pokémon like Pikachu.

Today, Meowth had a long metal pole. It had a special claw on the end. The Pokémon carefully used the pole to grab a red apple.

"Ha-ha," laughed Meowth. "Those noisemakers cannot stop me."

But Jessie and James could stop Meowth. Just as Meowth was about to take a bite, Jessie grabbed the apple from him. "Team Rocket always shares!" she cried.

Meowth grabbed the apple back

and hid it behind his back. "I was just about to split it three ways." The talking Pokémon pulled the apple out again.

"Hey!" cried Meowth.

"What is this?" Jessie cried.

Team Rocket stared at the apple. It had been eaten!

Jessie and James were angry. They thought Meowth had tricked them. "You ate it while we weren't looking," James said.

Just then, the noisemakers began ringing. Meowth was startled by the alarm.

"Run for it!" cried Jessie.

CHAPTER THREE

Caught Red-handed

“The alarms!” cried Ange.

Pikachu raced ahead to try to catch the thieves. It saw something in the trees. An apple fell to the ground. It had the same bite marks that the friends had seen before.

Pikachu kept running. At last, it found the thieves!

"*Pika pika!*" cried Pikachu. *I caught you!*

Three yellow Tiny Mouse Pokémon were holding apples. They looked like small Pikachu.

"*Pika pi!*" Ash's Pokémon wagged its finger. It was mad at them for taking Ange's fruit.

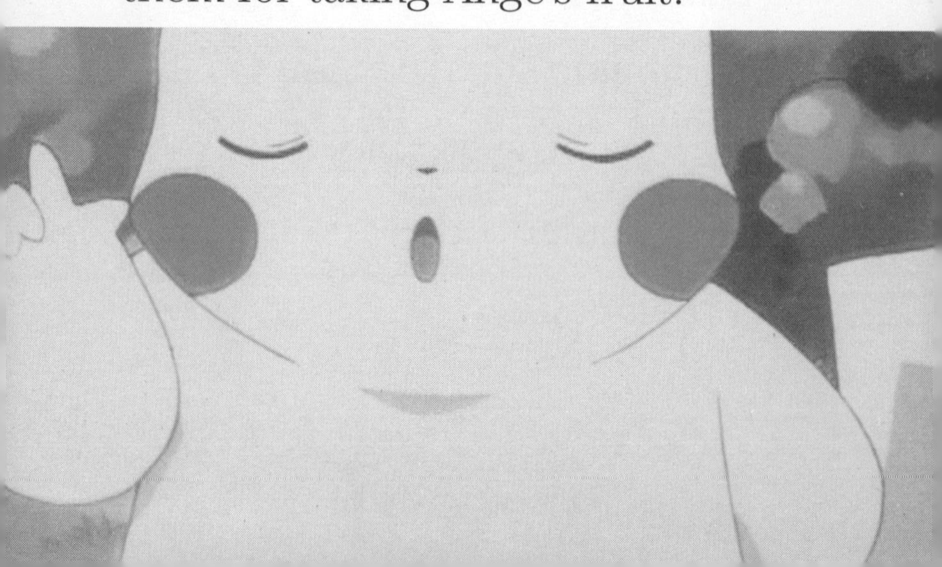

"*Pichuuu! Pichuuu!*" Pikachu heard tiny, sad voices call out from behind the trees. The tiny yellow Pokémon ran toward the sound.

Pikachu followed. It was surprised to find many Tiny Mouse Pokémon huddled together. The Pokémon looked very hungry. Now Pikachu understood why their friends had stolen the apples. They had nothing else to eat.

CHAPTER FOUR

Fearow Attack

In the sky, a Flying Pokémon circled the air. It was a Fearow.

"That Fearow has its eye on something," said Ange.

Ash was nervous. "That's the same direction Pikachu went! Let's

go!" he cried. Ash, Misty, Brock, and Ange ran into the forest, searching for Pikachu.

Soon enough, they found the herd of Pichu behind the bushes. The friends were surprised to find so many Pokémon.

Ash took Dexter, his Pokédex, out of his bag.

"Pichu, the Tiny Mouse Pokémon, is the first form of Pikachu," said Dexter. "The Pichu are Electric Pokémon. But they cannot control their electric power. The Pichu often shock themselves."

"So these Pichu were the fruit thieves," Ange said.

Just then, there was a screech from the sky. The Pichu watched the Fearow diving toward them. Its wings were spread wide. Its sharp claws opened and closed.

Three Pichu jumped to a branch. "*Pichuuu!*" cried the three Tiny Mouse Pokémon. Their bodies glowed with electricity. They shocked the Fearow. But they also shocked themselves. One by one, the three Pichu fell down.

The Fearow was stronger than the Pichu. It kept diving. On the ground, all of the tiny Pichu hugged one another. They were scared.

"*Pikachuuuu!*" Ash's Pokémon blasted a powerful Electric Shock.

It was not about to let this bully attack the tiny Pichu.

Electricity hit the Flying Pokémon with full force. The Fearow was stunned! With wings flapping, it turned and flew far away.

“Way to go, Pikachu!” cried Ash.

Pikachu smiled at its trainer. The Pichu smiled, too.

“*Pichu,*” they said. *Thank you, Pikachu.*

CHAPTER FIVE

The Poor Pichu

The Pichu returned the stolen fruit to Ange.

"*Pichu,*" the Pokémon said sadly. They were sorry.

"They are all hungry," said Brock.

"Those Pichu must have been

getting food for their friends," said Ash.

"Yes, I did hear there was not very much food in the forest this year," Ange replied.

"*Pika pika,*" Pikachu said sadly. He wanted Ange to give the Pichu the apples.

"Of course," smiled Ange. She

handed the fruit to the Pichu. "It is okay to eat," she told them.

The Pichu happily gobbled up the apples.

"They really love this fruit," said Ash.

"Yes." Ange sighed. "They will be back to eat more if we let them go."

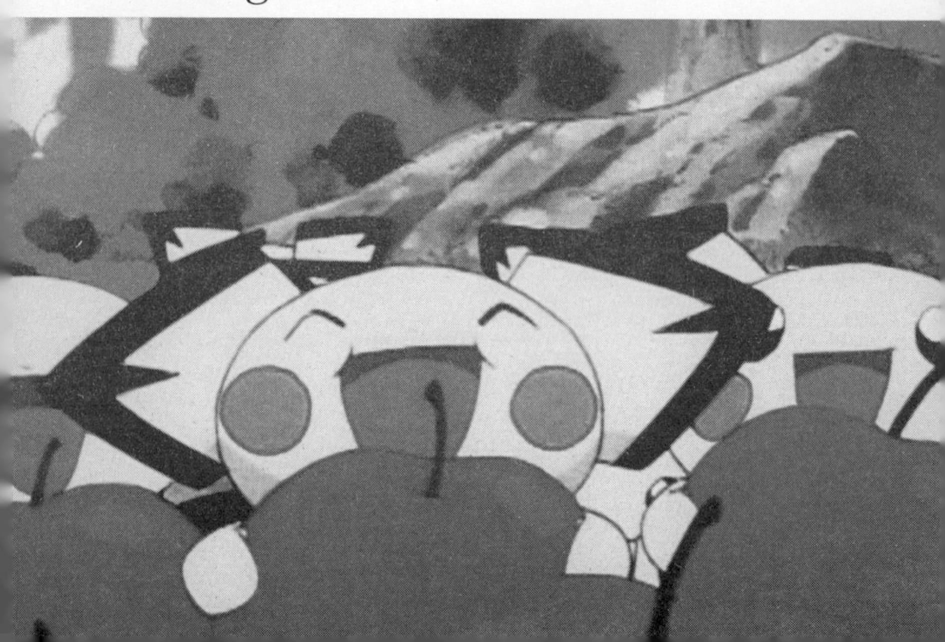

Pikachu frowned. The little yellow Pokémon wished there was a way for the Pichu and Ange to work things out.

"I know!" cried Ash. Pikachu smiled at its friend. Ash always had good ideas.

CHAPTER SIX

Team Rocket Trouble

Team Rocket flew over the orchard in their hot air balloon. Meowth rubbed its tummy happily.

"We can take enough fruit to fill our bellies," said Meowth.

"Let's steal some for the boss, too," said Jessie, smiling.

As Team Rocket dreamed about

eating the sweet apples, a flock of Pidgeys flew past the balloon.

"Huh?" Meowth watched the Bird Pokémon dive in a group. The Pidgey wanted apples, too. They were headed for the trees.

CHAPTER SEVEN

Team Pichu

In the orchard, Ash and Pikachu were teaching the Tiny Mouse Pokémon how to work together. Suddenly, they heard the flock of Pidgey flying near.

"Pikachu, now!" cried Ash.

Pikachu told a group of Pichu what to do. Quickly, they grouped

together. As a team, the Pichu shocked the Pidgey. But the Flying Pokémon kept diving.

Pikachu pointed to a second team of Pichu. They climbed the trees and leaped onto the Pidgeys' backs.

"*Pika!*" cried Pikachu. *Attack!*

The Pichu blasted the Flying Pokémon again. As the Pidgey flew away, the Pichu fell to the ground. They were dizzy from the Electric Shock, but they were happy. They had won the battle!

"The Pichu listened to Ash and Pikachu," said Ange.

"They are protecting the orchard to pay you back for the fruit," said Misty.

Pikachu smiled. It knew that the Pichu could help even more. Ash had a great plan.

"Okay, time for stage two. Show

them how it is done," Ash told Pikachu.

"*Pika!*" Pikachu showed the Pichu how to gather fruit for Ange. Some of the Pichu climbed the trees and picked the fruit. They dropped the apples to the Pichu below. The Pichu on the ground put the fruit in a box.

Ange was very pleased. "These Pichu are a great help. Perhaps things will work out, after all."

"Good work, everybody!" Ange told the Pichu. "Please eat as much fruit as you would like."

"*Pichu,*" smiled the Tiny Mouse Pokémon. *Thank you.*

CHAPTER EIGHT

Team Rocket Attacks

Soon, Team Rocket's hot air balloon was flying above Pikachu and its friends.

"Prepare for trouble," cried Jessie.

"Make it double," said James.

"What are you up to now?" yelled Ash.

“We are going to bring the boss a nice fruit basket!” Jessie laughed.

“Do not worry, Ange,” said Ash. “We will protect your orchard. Go get them, Pikachu!”

Pikachu jumped into the air,

ready to battle. Its cheeks sparked.

Just then, Meowth pushed a button. A long tube stretched out of the hot air balloon. It began to suck the air all around Pikachu.

"*Pika!*" cried the yellow Pokémon. It tried to get away, but the vacuum was too powerful. Pikachu was sucked toward the balloon.

"Pikachu!" cried Ash.

Now Pikachu was really mad. "*Pikachuuu!*" cried the little

yellow Pokémon. Its electric power blasted through the tube.

"Pikachu's electricity is powering our battery," Meowth laughed.

Poor Pikachu had no more strength. Now Team Rocket had stored up Pikachu's energy.

"Let's get the fruit," Jessie declared.

Meowth pushed a button.

Seven more long tubes stretched from the balloon basket.

"My eight-legged Octopus vacuum," smiled Meowth proudly. Suddenly, apples were being sucked into the tubes. They were disappearing faster and faster.

"Stop it!" cried Ash.

"Ange worked hard to grow this fruit," called Brock.

"Where are the Pichu?" cried Misty.

CHAPTER NINE

Pichu Power

The Pichu were angry, too. They climbed into the apple trees as fast as they could.

"The Pichu want to fight," said Brock.

All together, the Tiny Mouse Pokémon blasted Team Rocket.

The hot air balloon lit up with electricity. But the Pichu could not control the attack.

"Those silly things shocked themselves," said Meowth.

"Hurry and get the fruit before Pikachu gets its strength back," James said.

Meowth put the vacuum into reverse. Suddenly, the wind blasted the Pichu out of the trees and back to the ground.

"Pichu!" cried Ash. He was worried. He took out a Poké Ball.

Then Ange stopped him. "The Pichu are ready to fight again," she told Ash.

Determined, the Pichu marched back up the trees. They fought against the strong wind. One by one, they pushed one another higher. They climbed one on top of the other like a ladder until they reached their friend. They held onto Pikachu.

"It is like putting batteries together," said Brock. "The more of them there are, the more power there will be."

“That is great!” cheered Ange. She watched proudly as the Pichu burst with electricity. The power gave energy to Pikachu.

“All right!” said Ash. “Pikachu, Thunderbolt!”

Now Pikachu attacked Team

Rocket with more power than ever before. With the help of the Pichu, they overloaded Meowth's battery. Electricity flew everywhere.

"What is happening?" cried Jessie.

"The needle on my machine is way past full!" cried Meowth.

"It looks like Team Rocket is blasting off again!" cried Team Rocket together. The two teens and Meowth flew through the air and disappeared in the distance.

CHAPTER TEN

A Happy Harvest

Pikachu, the Pichu, and all of the apples fell back into the orchard.

"Pikachu!" cried Ash. Pikachu ran to its best friend.

The Pichu ran to Ange. "Are you all okay?" she asked, hugging them.

"*Pichu pichu!*" smiled the Pokémon. *We are fine.*

“Thanks for helping me,” Ange said. “We are going to work together from now on,” she told Ash, Misty, Brock, and Pikachu. “With the help of these little guys I will be able to guard the orchard much better than I could by myself.”

“That’s great!” Misty exclaimed.

But now it was time for the friends to continue their travels. Pikachu waved good-bye to its little friends.

"*Pichu!*" The Tiny Mouse Pokémon said good-bye. *We will miss you, Pikachu!*